HarperCollins®, 🏠®, and I Can Read Book® are
trademarks of HarperCollins Publishers Inc.

Dumpy's Apple Shop
Text and illustrations copyright © 2004 by Dumpy, LLC
Printed in the U.S.A. All rights reserved.
www.harperchildrens.com

Library of Congress Cataloging-in-Publication Data
Edwards, Julie, date
  Dumpy's apple shop / by Julie Edwards and Emma Walton Hamilton ; illustrated by
Tony Walton with Cassandra Boyd—1st ed.
    p.   cm.— (My first I can read book)
  "The Julie Andrews Collection."
  Summary: When Mrs. Barnes declares that "It's Apple Day," Dumpy wants to help
and finally gets his chance once all of the apples are picked and made into pies, apple
butter, and candy apples.
  ISBN 0-06-052692-0 — ISBN 0-06-052693-9 (lib. bdg.) — ISBN 0-06-052694-7
(pbk.)
  [1. Dump trucks—Fiction. 2. Trucks—Fiction. 3. Apples—Fiction.] I. Hamilton,
Emma Walton. II. Walton, Tony, ill. III. Boyd, Cassandra, ill. IV. Title. V. Series.
PZ7.E2562 Dw 2004
[E]—dc21   2003002336
                                                                                    CIP
                                                                                     AC

1   2   3   4   5   6   7   8   9   10
❖
First Edition

My First I Can Read Book®

Dumpy's Apple Shop

By Julie Andrews Edwards and Emma Walton Hamilton

Illustrated by Tony Walton

with Cassandra Boyd

HarperCollins*Publishers*

"It's Apple Day!"
said Mrs. Barnes.
"Today we sell our apples
in town.
Everyone will help."

3

"We need apples.

We need pies.

We need lots of apple butter,"

said Mrs. Barnes.

Charlie picked the apples.

Mrs. Barnes made the pies.

Dumpy wished
he could help.

Pop-Up made the apple butter.

Farmer Barnes made
candied apples.
Dumpy wished
he could help.

They put the apples in boxes.

They put the pies in boxes.

They put the apple butter in, too.

Dumpy SO wished he
could help!
Then they put the boxes
in Dumpy.

Now Dumpy was a big help!
"Broooom! Broooom!"
he said.

"Let's go!"

Everyone got into Dumpy.

Dumpy was very full.

Dumpy drove very slowly.

He drove very slowly to town.

Now they could
sell the apples.
But Dumpy still
wanted to help.

"Uh-oh!" said Farmer Barnes.

"We forgot our table.

How will we sell our apples?"

"Toot! Toot!" said Dumpy.

"Dumpy can be our table!"
said Charlie.

They put the apples in Dumpy.

They put the pies in Dumpy.

They put the apple butter
in, too.

They put a banner on Dumpy.

Dumpy was a happy
apple shop!

They sold the apples
and the pies.
They sold all the apple butter.

They sold lots of candied
apples too.

Everyone loved
Dumpy's shop!
Dumpy was a big help.

"There's one pie left for us!"
said Mrs. Barnes.
"Let's go home for dinner."

It was a happy Apple Day.